Dear Parent:
Your child's love of reading starts here!

Every child learns to read in a different way and at his or her own speed. Some go back and forth between reading levels and read favourite books again and again. Others read through each level in order. You can help your young reader improve and become more confident by encouraging his or her own interests and abilities. From books your child reads with you to the first books he or she reads alone, there are I Can Read Books for every stage of reading:

SHARED READING
Basic language, word repetition, and whimsical illustrations, ideal for sharing with your emergent reader

BEGINNING READING
Short sentences, familiar words, and simple concepts for children eager to read on their own

READING WITH HELP
Engaging stories, longer sentences, and language play for developing readers

READING ALONE
Complex plots, challenging vocabulary, and high-interest topics for the independent reader

ADVANCED READING
Short paragraphs, chapters, and exciting themes for the perfect bridge to chapter books

I Can Read Books have introduced children to the joy of reading since 1957. Featuring award-winning authors and illustrators and a fabulous cast of beloved characters, I Can Read Books set the standard for beginning readers.

A lifetime of discovery begins with the magical words "I Can Read!"

First published in Great Britain by HarperCollins Children's Books in 2008.
HarperCollins Children's Books is a division of HarperCollins Publishers Ltd.

1 3 5 7 9 10 8 6 4 2

ISBN-13: 978-0-00-726141-3
ISBN-10: 0-00-726141-1

Printed and bound in China

I Can Read!

BEGINNING
1
READING

Noddy's Pet Chicken

HarperCollins *Children's Books*

Noddy was driving Big-Ears
through Toyland.
It was a sunny day.

Big-Ears asked Noddy to slow down.

Noddy liked to drive fast

but did as Big-Ears asked.

"I listen when people tell me

what they want," said Noddy.

Suddenly they saw a chicken
standing in the road!

"Are you lost?" asked Big-Ears.

"Maybe I should take him home," said Noddy.

"I will give him my favourite foods and we'll play my favourite games."

"You funny little Noddy!"
said Big-Ears.

"I'm going to treat this chicken
very well," said Noddy.

He was so happy he sang a song:

"I'm a lucky boy,

Now I have a chicken.

He's my pet,

One I won't forget,

Now I have a chicken!"

Noddy put the chicken in the car
and began to drive very fast.
The chicken did not like riding
in the car.

"What is wrong, little chicken?"

asked Noddy.

Noddy drove more slowly.

"It will take forever

to get back to town!" he said.

Noddy drove to the Ice Cream Parlour
and bought two caramel treats.

He gave one caramel to the chicken.

"Go ahead and eat it!" said Noddy.

"It's good!"

But the chicken did not want to eat
the caramel treat.

Noddy saw Dinah Doll
and asked her why his chicken
would not eat the caramel treat.

"Maybe he likes a different kind
of treat," said Dinah.

Dinah gave the chicken some corn.

The chicken loved eating the corn.

"Not everybody likes to eat

the same things," said Dinah Doll.

"Now let's climb a tree!" cried Noddy
as he ran towards the tallest tree
in Toy Town Square.

The chicken looked up at Noddy.

It did not want to climb the tree.

"Now what can we do?"

said Noddy.

Then Noddy gave the chicken
some roller skates.
But the chicken did not know
how to roller skate.

The chicken did not want to do
any of Noddy's favourite things.
"What do you want to do?" he asked.

Noddy threw a ball for the chicken.
But the chicken did not want
to play fetch.

Bumpy Dog saw the ball.

He wanted to play fetch.

He ran towards the ball

and scared the chicken.

Mr Plod saw the chicken running.

He did not like chickens.

"Noddy, take the chicken home!"

Mr Plod ordered.

Noddy asked Big-Ears for advice.

Big-Ears always knows what to do.

Big-Ears told Noddy

that chickens do not like to do

the same things that people do.

"I only thought about what I wanted

to do," said Noddy.

"We should bring the chicken
back to where we found it.
Then he might remember
where he belongs," said Big-Ears.

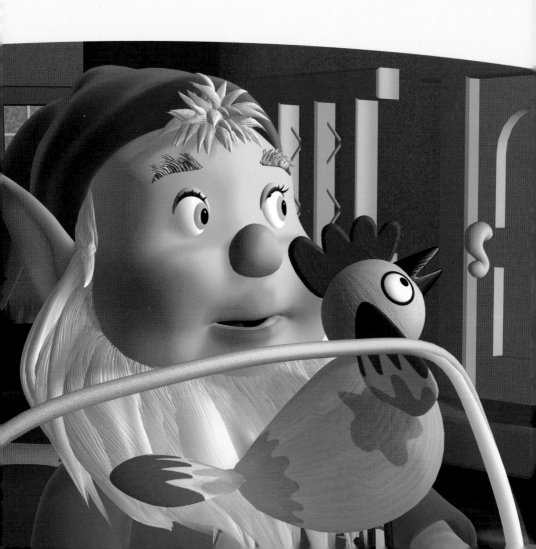

The chicken flew out of Noddy's car
towards a garden with a pink fence.
"This must be his home!" said Noddy.

"If you want the chicken to be happy, you must let him go home," said Big-Ears.

"I want what is best for him.

Go home, chicken!

I will miss you!" said Noddy.

Tessie Bear was standing

in the garden.

"You found my lost chicken!" she cried.

"Thank you for bringing him back."

"Now I can feed him corn
and let him scratch the grass.
Those are his favourite things to do,"
said Tessie Bear.

"So that is what chickens like to do!"
Noddy was pleased to find out.

Noddy and Big-Ears waved goodbye
to Tessie Bear and the chicken.
"Things have turned out best
for everybody," they smiled.

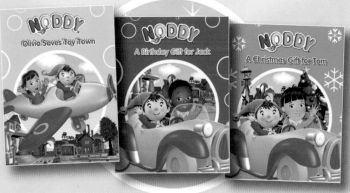